THE
MAGICAL
UNICORN
SOCIETY

OFFICIAL
HANDBOOK

Feiwel and Friends
New York

With special thanks to Jonny Leighton

A Feiwel and Friends Book
An imprint of Macmillan Publishing Group, LLC
175 Fifth Avenue, New York, NY 10010

Our books may be purchased in bulk for promotional, educational, or business use. Please contact your
local bookseller or the Macmillan Corporate and Premium Sales Department at (800) 221-7945 ext. 5442 or
by e-mail at MacmillanSpecialMarkets@macmillan.com.

ISBN 978-1-250-20619-0 (hardcover) / ISBN 978-1-250-21343-3

Book design by Sophie Erb and Claire Cater
Cover design by Angie Allison
Feiwel and Friends logo designed by Filomena Tuosto

Originally published in Great Britain by Michael O'Mara Books Limited

First published in the United States by Feiwel and Friends, an imprint of Macmillan

First U.S. edition, 2018

5 7 9 10 8 6
mackids.com

THE
MAGICAL
UNICORN
SOCIETY

OFFICIAL
HANDBOOK

Written by Selwyn E. Phipps

Illustrated by Harry and Zanna Goldhawk

with additional illustrations by Helen Dardik

CONTENTS

About the
AUTHOR

Greetings! My name is Selwyn E. Phipps and I am the current president of the Magical Unicorn Society. My friends call me Selwyn – and so should you. If you have picked up this book, I am guessing that you are a fan of unicorns and, if this is the case, I think we shall get on tremendously well.

Before we begin, let me tell you something of myself. I first became interested in unicorns as a boy. My mother was a keen explorer who travelled the world to discover all she could about these magical creatures. When I was little, she would sit me down by the fire on cold evenings and tell me spellbinding tales of her journeys. I dreamed that one day I would follow in her footsteps.

Some years later, my dream came true when I landed a job as a fact-finder for the Magical Unicorn Society. I embarked on many daring expeditions: climbing mountains, crossing deserts and navigating swamps just to catch a glimpse of a

Mountain Jewel unicorn or a Desert Flame. During my career, I have been fortunate enough to encounter creatures from each of the seven unicorn families that exist in the world today.

As the 101st president of the Society, and with my adventuring days behind me, I'm ready to pass on the tales I have heard and the experiences I have enjoyed. So, I would suggest you make yourself comfortable because there is a lot to discover and learn. If you believe in unicorns, that is ...

Selwyn

101ST PRESIDENT OF THE
MAGICAL UNICORN SOCIETY

Est. 1577

What is the MAGICAL UNICORN SOCIETY?

The Magical Unicorn Society unites people across the globe who love unicorns. The job of the men and women of the Society is to document everything there is to know about these unique creatures and to protect them whenever they are in need. We track unicorns in their natural habitats, document our encounters with them, study their ways and record the stories that surround them. So if you do want to find out everything there is to know about unicorns, you've come to the right place. (OK – we know *nearly* everything. Mustn't boast!)

The Society has branches all around the world, from Paris to Madrid, Hong Kong to Tokyo and New York to Buenos Aires. My local branch is in a snug little place called Silver Square, an old building nestled among the cosy Victorian terraces of South London. It is, for now, the headquarters of the whole organization. However, the headquarters have been in many different locations around the world during the Society's long history.

Silver Square houses the Society's great library, which contains all the knowledge handed down over the centuries by our intrepid and dedicated members. The earliest documents in the library date back to Ancient Egyptian times. The pharaohs of the day wanted to know more about the Desert Flame unicorns that they saw trekking across the Sahara. They sent warriors to capture the unicorns and tame them. But of course this was foolish: unicorns cannot be tamed. Luckily, the pharaohs also tasked their brightest scholars with understanding these mystical creatures from a distance. The papyrus scrolls on which they recorded their findings are stored safely in the library to this day.

Over the years, many different people have come into contact with unicorns. A fearless Viking queen known as Thora the Brave formed a special bond with a wounded Ice Wanderer which she came across in the snowy wastelands of the north. She lost three fingers to frostbite on that fateful trip, but nevertheless wrote down all she discovered about these solitary creatures. Then there was the young king, named Dagobert, who lived in medieval France, who once encountered a beautiful Woodland Flower travelling through his kingdom. Unfortunately for the arrogant and vain Dagobert, the encounter didn't go quite as he'd hoped.

But it wasn't until the 16th century, in Renaissance Italy, that the Magical Unicorn Society was officially formed by Luca di Bosco and Alessandra Massima. They devoted their lives to gathering unicorn lore, and together they wrote and illustrated the first encyclopedia dedicated entirely to unicorns.

So you see, we have had many illustrious and noble members in our ranks over the centuries, as well as countless brave and fearless explorers. Today's members are dedicated to the same task as their predecessors. As a society, we've never been stronger, but we can always do more. That's why we are telling our story now, in the hope that we may inspire a new generation of people to respect and protect unicorns for decades to come.

Let's get lost in the land of unicorns...

DISCOVERING UNICORNS

For as long as there have been humans, there have been unicorns, too. In fact, unicorns lived here on Earth eons before we did.

The Gold Unicorn and the Silver Unicorn are believed to have been the first of their kind. They existed back when the world was young, and magical creatures were as common as clouds in the sky. All sorts of enchanted beings lived on Earth at this time, from fleet-footed fairies to colonies of mischievous nymphs, and ice-breathing dragons that could freeze anything in their path. Unlike the Gold Unicorn and the Silver Unicorn, many of these magical creatures still exist today – if you know where to find them.

When humans appeared, they came into contact with unicorns and, at first, they lived in harmony together. However, things changed as people spread across the Earth, increasing in number and gaining powers of a different kind: mechanical, electrical, industrial. Humans came to rely on modern technologies and fewer people remembered the old magic. As the world grew busier and noisier, unicorns also became shyer creatures. They retreated to the highest mountains and deep into the thickest woods, where they used their intimate knowledge of the landscape and highly developed camouflage to hide themselves.

Over the decades, their magical powers evolved and became more specialized. Some unicorns have manes that can make them invisible at will. This allows them to roam unseen and without fear of harm. Others can fly, and anyone who tries to sneak up on them will find that they can disappear in the blink of an eye.

Because they are so hard to find, many people believe unicorns only exist in fairy tales. But we at the Society know that unicorns are real. There are seven types in the world today – Mountain Jewels, Water Moons, Woodland Flowers, Desert Flames, Ice Wanderers, Storm Chasers and Shadow Nights. On the following pages you will find a map of where in the world they have been seen.

WHERE IN THE WORLD?

NORTH AMERICA

ATLANTIC OCEAN

PACIFIC OCEAN

SOUTH AMERICA

KEY

MOUNTAIN JEWELS

WOODLAND FLOWERS

DESERT FLAMES

STORM CHASERS

WATER MOONS

ICE WANDERERS

SHADOW NIGHTS

1
BUENOS AIRES

2
PHOENIX

Unicorns now wander far and wide, but these are the main centres of their original habitats. This map also includes notable Society buildings in existence today.

EUROPE

ASIA

PACIFIC OCEAN

AFRICA

INDIAN OCEAN

AUSTRALIA AND OCEANIA

SOUTHERN OCEAN

4

3

5

3 ISTANBUL

4 LONDON

5 TOKYO

The Myth *of the* Gold Unicorn *and the* Silver Unicorn

The first-ever unicorns existed so far back in time that the Magical Unicorn Society has to rely on tales told around campfires by the earliest nomadic humans for any information about them. There have been many different stories since, but one thing that remains constant is that the first two unicorns in the world were a beautiful gold and a stunning silver.

The stories always begin in the distant, misty past, beside a magical river in the heart of the Himalayas. So many magical beings had sprung from this river that the surrounding hills were crowded with creatures of all shapes and sizes. There were double-winged birds that could fly to the edge of the atmosphere and luminous moths that lit up the night like exploding stars. Not all the magical beings were beautiful or good. The cruellest creatures of all were the Winter Dragons.

These beasts were ten metres long, with huge, sail-like wings. They were covered in shiny ice-blue scales, had eyes like sapphires and tails like metal whips. They lived in caves deep within the mountains, only emerging to hunt. Unlike other dragons, the Winter Dragons didn't breathe fire, but an icy inferno that froze their victims to the spot. The dragons could easily snatch up their defenceless prey and devour it in one gulp.

The Winter Dragons were a deadly menace for all the creatures that lived in the meadows beneath the mountains. They were regularly attacked by the dragons, and lived in fear. Yet, for

a pair of horses who grazed there, a chance encounter with a Winter Dragon would change their lives in an unexpected way.

One evening, the two horses were nibbling on the lush grass and berries growing in the meadow. The Sun was beginning to dip towards the horizon and the air glowed purple and gold. Suddenly, out of this beautiful sky, a nightmarish dragon reared into view. The tawny-brown female horse and the snowy-grey male turned to run as the Winter Dragon swooped down for the kill.

The scaly monster blasted the landscape with its icy breath, leaving trees and shrubs encased in thick frost. The horses whinnied in fear, kicked up their hooves and galloped desperately towards the mountains. Despite being treacherous territory for horses, it was their only hope of escape.

As the horses climbed, the air grew bitterly cold and their hooves slipped on the rocks. The tawny-brown horse spotted a rocky outcrop and darted towards it. The silver-grey horse

followed, and together they huddled underneath it. Shielded by the rock, they were protected, but completely trapped.

The Winter Dragon blasted the horses, freezing their tails, but its huge claws couldn't get hold of them. The winged beast roared and lurched skywards once more. The horses seized their chance and galloped as fast as they could along a mountain pass, towards a raging waterfall – where the river's magic was strongest.

The roar of the falls was immense and a thick mist swirled and frothed around the cliff side. The horses realized that to get to the other side of the pass they had no option but to plunge through the cascading waters. But they need not have been afraid – the river never harmed an animal with a good heart, or one in need. And no animals had ever been in greater need than they.

As the Sun touched the horizon, which is a particularly magical time of day, the horses charged through the waterfall. Inside the thrashing falls, neither horse could see a thing; all they could

do was keep going. Then something magical happened. The last ray of sunshine bounced off the waterfall and a transformation occurred. When they stepped out the other side, they were no longer horses. They were unicorns.

The tawny-brown horse had become golden from head to tail. Its new horn shone as brightly as the Sun. The white-grey horse had become silver, with a dazzling coat like the reflected moon and a pale silver horn. They had grown bigger and stronger, and they were about to find out they had amazing, special powers.

But the unicorns didn't have time to reflect on their change because the Winter Dragon was upon them. As they rushed away from the magical waterfall and on to a snowy mountain ledge, the dragon attacked. When its ghastly jaws were just a hair's breadth from their necks, the Silver Unicorn stamped its hoof on the ground. In an instant, the silver of its coat grew even brighter, blinding the dragon. Then the Golden Unicorn stamped its hoof and a huge wall of snow surged down the mountain. The avalanche battered into the side of the dragon, sweeping it off the mountainside and into the abyss below.

The two new unicorns were stunned, but discovered they
had still more magical powers. They were able to move
sure-footedly at great speed across the mountainside and
could make themselves invisible at will. Gone were the days
of fearing the Winter Dragons.

Over the coming days their magic grew until the unicorns gained
complete control of their powers. They became confident enough
to leave the enchanted plains and wander the Earth. Each time
they found a suitable location, they would bow their heads and
touch the ground with their horns. In an instant, a new family
of unicorns would spring from the spot. A family of unicorns
is called a blessing and each new blessing they created was
wonderfully unique. In this way, the seven families of unicorns
arrived and established themselves in lands stretching from
the icy north to the sweltering desert sands.

The Lore of the Gold Unicorn and the Silver Unicorn

UNIQUE QUALITY

The Gold Unicorn and the Silver Unicorn were the first unicorns to appear at a time when the Earth was full of magic.

HORNS

One had a horn of glistening gold and the other of pale silver.

APPEARANCE

These unicorns had sleek, short-haired coats and manes woven with delicate strands of gold or silver.

HABITAT

They lived in lush valleys, in the shadow of tall mountains.

MAGIC

Invisibility • Ability to produce shockwaves and light • Speed • Power to bring new unicorns into the world

WISDOM

The Gold Unicorn and the Silver Unicorn represent new life.

UNICORN FOOD

Unicorns have big appetites and their basic diet consists of grass, plants, flowers and berries. However, as with humans, a unicorn's diet varies depending on its habitat. This visual guide introduces some of the most common unicorn foods.

COLD TERRAINS

The unicorns who inhabit icy landscapes must forage
under the snow to find the nutrients they need.

Bearberries
These help keep
unicorns warm.

Red Algae
This plant is full
of vitamins for a
healthy coat.

Diamond Leaf
Willow
This builds speed
and agility.

Arctic Poppies
These strengthen the unicorns'
eyesight, much needed for
those long, dark winters.

MOUNTAIN TERRAINS

Mountain ranges provide an abundance of
plants and flowers for unicorns to feast on.

Boston Ivy
This is the ideal plant
to keep a Mountain Jewel
unicorn looking shiny
and healthy.

Himalayan Onions
The leaves of this plant are
perfect for toughening hooves.

Yellow and White Orchids
These flowers help
strengthen muscle,
important for a
unicorn's balance on
mountain slopes.

Sheep's Bit
This is a tasty
unicorn treat.

WARM TERRAINS

Arid land and blistering heat mean desert unicorns have
to be clever to find the foods they need to survive.

Silver Torch Cactus

These cacti are full of water and
nutrients – Desert Flames use their
horns to break them open.

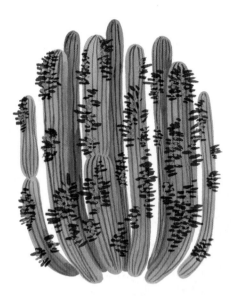

Scorpion Weed

These are good for
a healthy heart.

Agave

These enhance a
unicorn's hearing.

Sacred Datura

This plant is poisonous to
all creatures except unicorns.
It provides a quick energy
boost for a blessing.

WATERY TERRAINS

Unicorns that live near oceans, lakes and rivers
have a huge variety of food to choose from.

Winky Wooh
This gives just the right boost
to a unicorn's magical powers.

Marigolds
These sugary petals
are a special treat.

Dwarf Water Lilies
These are great for speed
and flexibility.

Pink Lotus
The seed heads are perfect
for protection from the Sun.

Mountain Jewels

Mountain Jewel unicorns are strong, fierce
and resilient. They have to be, as they are found
in some of the harshest environments on Earth.
From the Himalayas to the Andes, and from the Alps
to the Hindu Kush, these unicorns survive and thrive.

Mountain Jewel unicorns are capable of travelling huge distances across rocky and icy terrain, as well as surviving at very high altitude and through cold, brutal winters.

There is some variation in their colouration and appearance across their different habitats. In South America, Mountain Jewels are a pale, dove grey, with splashes of dusty pink across their bodies and manes. They have thick, shaggy coats for extra warmth and beautiful coral horns. They use these horns as beacons at night, sending out pink light through the skies to communicate with other unicorns across vast distances. They are inclined to solitude and wander alone across the salt flats and foothills in search of food and shelter.

In contrast, the Mountain Jewels of Central Asia are more sociable creatures. They travel together in blessings of at least five or six unicorns, but there are stories of these herds reaching up to a hundred in number. Their territory is enormous. In the spring and summer they can be found travelling across the Central Asian steppe, a massive area of grassland perfect for grazing. But as the year turns, they make their way south to the long mountain ranges of the Hindu Kush and the Himalayas, where they live among rocky clifftops.

Central Asian Mountain Jewels are a tawny, light brown colour, and some have dark, spotted patches on their coats. Their horns are made of beautiful brown opal, a dark stone, which is flecked with blues, pinks and greens. Rather than emitting light, these horns radiate warmth.

Mountain Jewels are known to be one of the gruffer unicorn species. They are hardy, no-nonsense animals. They can trek to the point where other animals would die of exhaustion and just keep on going. These unicorns fight and quarrel among themselves, and even butt horns together in annoyance. Quite what they have to be cross about is hard to say. Perhaps all that time spent with their families and herds gets on their nerves.

I have seen magnificent Mountain Jewels fighting with my own eyes. As a young man, I was trekking through Nepal when I came across two young males battling with each other. They didn't see me, as I was hiding behind a rock. When they clacked horns together, colourful sparks flew off in all directions, like a rainbow-coloured sparkler on Bonfire Night. Eventually, I sneezed and they spotted me – an embarrassing mistake on my part. They stopped fighting and dashed off down the mountainside without a backward glance.

After my trek, I spent some time at a temple with a learned scholar and fellow society member named Ditya Giri, who told me about the local legend of the Mountain Jewels. She showed me a mural painted on a wall inside the temple that depicted the Battle of the Shining Jewels, which had taken place over a thousand years before near the mountain city of Mandu.

Back then, Mandu was a trading city, selling goods such as silk, spices, fruit and vegetables. But what made it a special city lay in the mountains beyond its walls where there were mines bursting with precious jewels – corals, opals, pearls, sapphires and diamonds. The citizens were grateful for the jewels that made them rich, and knew that they owed this wealth to the Mountain Jewel unicorns that lived in the mountains.

Centuries before, the city folk had begun to worship the Mountain Jewels. Some people even tried to live among the unicorns. It took years for trust to develop between the unicorns and those people, who became known as 'Whisperers'.

However, eventually the unicorns not only accepted them, but also showed them the hidden jewel mines, full of riches.

Naturally, many people in neighbouring cities were jealous of Mandu's wealth, and the city became a target for bandits. One night a gang of robbers set fire to part of the city wall. The flames spread quickly and soon the great wooden gate that protected the city was completely destroyed. When the fire eventually died down, Mandu was ravaged by the bandits, who looted it to the last diamond.

When the city folk were able to regroup, they sent out a battalion of Mandu's finest warriors. The soldiers chased the bandits through the mountains and down onto the grassy foothills. Eventually, the army and the bandits faced each other on the desolate plains. The Battle of the Shining Jewels was fought for fifteen long days and there were terrible casualties on both sides. By the sixteenth day it looked as if all was lost for Mandu.

The generals called for the Whisperers to pray for the dead and dying soldiers. The Whisperers solemnly conducted the Invocation of the Mountain Jewel Unicorns. As they recited this magical prayer, something phenomenal occurred. Those who had fallen in battle were filled with the spirit of the unicorns and transformed into Mountain Jewels.

With their ranks replenished with these newly formed unicorns, the soldiers of Mandu went into battle once more. The power of the unicorns ensured victory on their side. They easily vanquished the bandits and reclaimed the riches of their city. The soldiers who survived returned to rebuild the city, and those who were lost and transformed joined the Mountain Jewel blessing, roaming freely with them on the mountainsides.

The city of Mandu has seen its fortunes ebb and flow over the years, as Ditya Giri told me. However, its fate has always been intertwined with that of Mountain Jewel unicorns. That is why it is such an important centre of learning for the Magical Unicorn Society and a favourite destination for its scholars to this day.

The Lore of Mountain Jewels

UNIQUE QUALITY

Mountain Jewels are the strongest and toughest
unicorns. They are fiercely loyal to each other.

HORNS

Central Asian Mountain Jewels have tightly curled
horns of solid opal. The horns of South American
Mountain Jewels look similar but are made of coral.

APPEARANCE

South American Mountain Jewels have thick, dove-grey
coats with flecks of coral pink. Their cousins in Central
Asia have tawny coats with dark patches.

HABITAT

These unicorns are found in mountainous regions.
They can survive freezing temperatures and icy winds.

MAGIC

Can emit warmth or light from their horns
• Stamina • Have unnaturally long lives

WISDOM

Mountain Jewels are associated
with prosperity, courage
and perseverance.

If you believe, you
will start to notice the
presence of unicorns
all around, like a fog
lifting and sunlight
illuminating the land.

UNICORN SYMBOLOGY

Throughout history, unicorns have been used in images to symbolize values and communicate ideas. Their essence and beauty have lent themselves to striking pictures found around the world – from royal crests to breathtaking works of art.

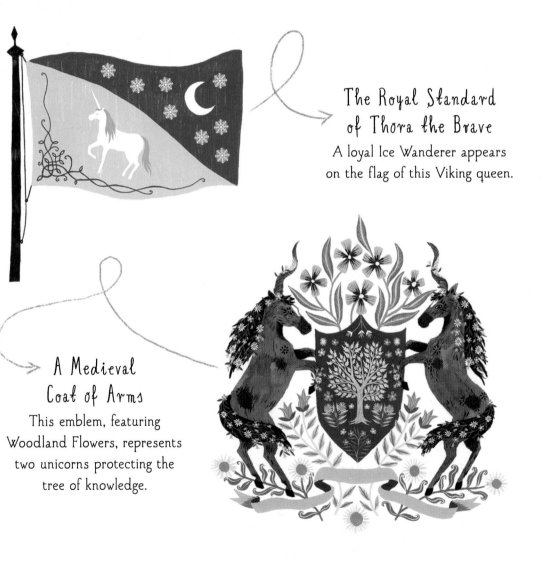

The Royal Standard of Thora the Brave

A loyal Ice Wanderer appears on the flag of this Viking queen.

A Medieval Coat of Arms

This emblem, featuring Woodland Flowers, represents two unicorns protecting the tree of knowledge.

The Magical Unicorn Society's Official Crest

Unicorns appearing on crests and coats of arms represent power and prestige.

Est. 1577

Unicorn imagery in Greek art

Water Moons and Shadow Nights were known to ancient civilizations, and have been represented on pottery and in artwork.

Desert Flames in tomb paintings

Ancient Egyptians included Desert Flames in pictures painted on the walls of tombs.

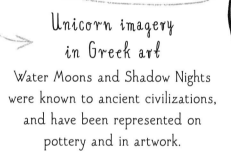

Shadow Night statue

Shadow Nights appear in reality and dreams, but many artists have tried to capture them in sculpture. Some statues are believed to carry a curse.

Water Moons

Water Moon unicorns are strange, water-dwelling creatures, almost the polar opposite of their land-living cousins, Mountain Jewels. They are incredibly difficult to spot. The only time they are visible is on clear nights when they can be seen by the light of the moon and stars.

Water Moon unicorns are often found on the banks of major rivers across the world, from the Nile in Egypt and the Thames in England to the Yangtze in China and the Ganges in India. They can also be seen around the Great Lakes of North America and on the shores of large oceans, such as the Pacific Ocean on the shores of San Francisco. They feature in folktales about ghostly water-dwelling horses, but Water Moons mean no harm and they are certainly not ghosts.

These unicorns don't just live near water – they live in it. Throughout history, sailors have told tales of seeing them out at sea during treacherous storms, galloping through the waves. Water Moons are friends to seafarers, guiding ships home on dark, stormy nights.

Water Moons have the longest tails and manes in the unicorn world. Their tails reach the ground – or water – and when they are racing at full gallop, their manes fly back the length of their bodies. River-dwelling unicorns tend to be white-blonde in colour, with horns of shimmering crystal, whereas unicorns who live in oceans and lakes are pale blue, with dark sapphire horns. Their horns are used as beacons, lighting up to warn or guide stranded sailors, much like the beam of a lighthouse.

It was a young Italian painter, Luca di Bosco, who first discovered what makes Water Moons so special. His discovery led to the creation of the Magical Unicorn Society.

Luca was born in Italy in the middle of the 16th century – an extraordinary time for art, science, medicine and exploration. A scientist called Galileo Galilei was about to re-write the rules of astronomy, and an artist named Michelangelo had recently created an incredible painting on the ceiling of the Sistine Chapel in the Vatican. Luca also dreamed of becoming a famous artist one day.

He left his hometown and travelled to Venice, where he became an apprentice painter. He trained for years, perfecting his techniques and exploring the canal-lined city. Venice was a trade hub, and wealthy merchants came from all around the world to buy paintings and decorative pottery.

One night, Luca was walking through the streets of Venice when he realized he was being followed. The twisting alleys beside the canals were notoriously full of thieves. When two pickpockets caught up with him, they pounced. One snatched Luca's money and the other gave him a hammer-blow punch to the jaw, which sent him tumbling into the canal.

Luca plunged deep into the water and, unable to swim, began to sink beneath the murky depths. As panic turned to desperation, he noticed a strange light flickering on the canal floor. The light grew stronger and Luca thought he could see an animal appearing through the gloom – was it a horse? Exhausted and delirious, Luca passed out, but not before he glimpsed a shining crystal horn protruding from the creature's head.

When he regained consciousness, Luca found himself slumped on the path beside the canal. Somehow he had cheated death. The streets were empty. Who had helped him? Had he been saved by the strange underwater creature? That seemed to be the only explanation, but it couldn't possibly be true. The creature had looked a lot like a unicorn – something Luca thought only existed in myths.

Luca recovered from his ordeal, but he was forever changed by it. He began painting the horned creature he had seen in the canal and it featured in what would become his most famous masterpiece. He also began having strange visions of the future – of travelling to distant lands and meeting others who had encountered these elusive creatures.

One day, when he was working in his studio, one of his visions came true. A woman called Alessandra Massima came to his

door. She introduced herself and explained that she, too, had
seen a unicorn. She was a merchant traveller from Florence and
a book-binder. Through her work she had seen one of Luca's
unicorn paintings and it had led her to him. She explained that the
creature he painted was a Water Moon unicorn. She was planning
an expedition to discover more about these magical creatures and
wanted him to come with her.

Luca was stunned. He'd had visions of travelling to strange
lands and now here was a woman offering him the chance to
do just that. Luca didn't hesitate. He packed up his belongings
and joined Alessandra on her merchant ship. They sailed to
the four corners of the Earth trying to discover other sightings
and encounters with Water Moons. Their studies proved that
any human who gets close to this kind of unicorn experiences
dreams and visions in which they can see what the future holds.

By the time Luca and Alessandra returned to Venice, rich and
successful explorers, they had seen many varieties of unicorn
and heard all sorts of ancient tales about them. They dedicated
their lives to compiling this knowledge, creating a library of
books written and bound by Alessandra and illustrated with
Luca's wonderful paintings. And so, the Magical Unicorn Society,
as we know it today, was born.

The Lore of Water Moons

UNIQUE QUALITY

Water Moons live exclusively in and around water.

HORNS

Water Moons that live in rivers have clear,
crystal horns while Water Moons that live
in oceans or lakes have horns of sapphire.

APPEARANCE

They have the longest tails and manes of all the unicorns.
The river Water Moons have white coats while the Water
Moons of oceans and lakes have pale-blue coats.

HABITAT

These unicorns are found in rivers, lakes and oceans.

MAGIC

Can give humans they encounter the ability
to see into the future • Invisibility (unless
they are seen by the light of the moon)

WISDOM

Water Moons represent the
mysteries of time.

The

A to Z of

UNICORNS

A IS FOR ANCIENT

Unicorns have been galloping around the Earth for thousands of years and were here long before humans.

B IS FOR BLESSING

The collective name for a group of unicorns.

C IS FOR COATS

Each unicorn family has a different type of coat. Some shimmer in the moonlight and others glow in the sunshine.

D IS FOR DREAMS

Some unicorns have the power to control human dreams. They can give the dreamer visions of the future.

E IS FOR THE ELEMENTS

Storm Chaser unicorns have magical control over lightning, thunder, rain and sunshine.

F IS FOR FRIENDSHIP

Bonding with unicorns is rare but, if you do, you'll be friends for life.

G IS FOR GRACEFUL

Beautiful to watch, unicorns move with skill and care.

H IS FOR HORNS

Unicorns' horns are made of precious materials, such as coral, opal and silver. Many unicorns have horns that glow.

I IS FOR INVISIBLE

Unicorns are shy creatures who can become invisible when they don't want to be seen.

J IS FOR JUSTICE

Unicorns are fair, kind and respectful creatures.

K IS FOR KINSHIP

Family is very important to unicorns – they are incredibly loyal to their magical brothers and sisters.

L IS FOR LEGENDS

Unicorns have appeared throughout history and are the subject of many myths and legends.

M IS FOR MAGIC

All unicorns have magical powers, some can fly and others are incredibly strong.

N IS FOR NIGHT

Unicorns often use the cloak of darkness to move around freely. Shadow Nights only exist after dark.

O IS FOR OMEN

Some people believe that seeing a unicorn is an omen, or a clue, to what might happen in the future.

P IS FOR PLANTS

Unicorns are vegetarians. They eat plants such as Red Algae and Winky Woohs.

Q IS FOR QUICK

Unicorns are quick-witted, fleet of foot and quick to help.

R IS FOR ROYALTY

Because of their dignified and proud personalities, unicorns are often used as symbols for royalty.

S IS FOR SONG

Legend has it that the shy Woodland Flower unicorns can be summoned by song.

T IS FOR TELEPATHIC

Some unicorn species can talk to each other, and to humans, using only their minds.

U IS FOR UNIQUE

There are no magical creatures quite like the unicorn.

V IS FOR VICTORY

In many legends, unicorns are the good force that conquers evil.

W IS FOR WISDOM

Unicorns are wise animals and each family passes knowledge down through the generations.

X IS FOR X-HOOF PRINT

X is the shape a Shadow Night's hoof makes on the ground.

Y IS FOR YOUNGLING

This is the name given to a baby unicorn.

Z IS FOR ZEN

The feeling of calm felt when someone has encountered a unicorn.

Woodland
Flowers

The Château de Temps was once a beautiful castle,
home to a kind-hearted dynasty of medieval
kings and queens. It stood on a French hillside,
surrounded by a deep forest. Its towers were
tall and magnificent. Colourful banners
adorned its walls and beautiful
flowers grew in the gardens.

Then one day a cold, cruel and mean-spirited man named Dagobert came to the throne. He treated neighbouring kingdoms with contempt. War ravaged the land and the château was brought to its knees. The Château de Temps became a dark shadow of its former self, squatting on the hillside like a poisonous toad.

One day the local people, who were regularly forced to entertain the king, put on a play about the enchanted forest that surrounded the château. It told of a magical tree with golden leaves that grew in the depths of the woods. Great power and long life was promised to anyone who picked these leaves. Dagobert, seized by desire, set out the next day in search of the tree.

He took with him his trusted servant, Antoine, a brave and kind young man who was forced to withstand many cruel words and deeds from his master. Antoine had played in the forest as a boy and knew it and its creatures well. He warned the king of the dangerous enchantments that befell anyone who strayed too far inside, but his warnings fell on deaf ears.

As night drew on, Antoine pitched a tent for the king and they settled down to sleep. But their slumbers were troubled by strange animal noises and a restless breeze that made it sound like the trees were whispering to each other.

For several days they continued on their quest. When their provisions grew low, Dagobert announced he would hunt for more food. Antoine begged him not to kill any living creature in the forest and instead survive on the plentiful nuts and berries that could be found there, but the king ignored him. Dagobert loved hunting. Soon he was very excited to find himself on the trail of some mysterious, heart-shaped hoof prints.

The tracks led to a clearing in the forest, where Dagobert came across a beautiful creature. It was shaped like a horse, but bigger and more graceful. Its coat was a deep brown and velvety. It had a single, twisted horn that protruded proudly from its forehead and its mane was laced with wild flowers. It was a unicorn. Dagobert imagined how impressive its head would look hanging above his fireplace.

Raising his bow, he took aim. Just as he was about to let the string loose, Dagobert felt an urgent hand on his arm. "Stop, I beg you, Sir," Antoine gasped. "It's a magical creature ..."

"Treachery!" Dagobert spat, determined to punish Antoine's impertinence. But something made him stop. The unicorn was looking at them with its deep brown eyes. Something strange was in the air ... *magic*. There was a chattering, chirruping and squawking all around them. Dagobert and Antoine became aware of a multitude of eyes watching them: squirrels, foxes, birds, mice and deer. The air chilled and the sky turned dark.

Suddenly, the unicorn spoke. "Beware the Golden Tree," it warned. Then, as quickly as they'd appeared, the unicorn and all the other animals melted back into the forest.

"Heed this warning, Sir. That was a Woodland Flower unicorn," Antoine implored. But Dagobert just smiled. The unicorn and its strange magic only proved to him how desirable the leaves from the Golden Tree must be.

They spent the next day searching and entered a more promising area of the forest. Magic hung heavily in the air, and the forest floor teemed with insects as bright as jewels. The trees seemed to sway and bow in greeting. Just as the Sun rose on the seventh day, Dagobert saw a glint of gold in a clearing ahead. The magical tree stood in front of him, dazzling in the morning light.

Dagobert reached out and plucked a heavy golden leaf. As he did this, there was a deep sigh from the tree's branches and Dagobert felt magic seep from the leaf into his bones. He felt powerful, wise – immortal.

However, as a malevolent grin spread across his face, Dagobert didn't notice the delicate roots that had begun to sprout from his feet. His arms and legs grew stiff and rough to the touch. His hair turned green and unfurled like a plant stretching out after winter. By the time that Dagobert realized what was happening it was far too late. He was rooted to the spot.

Antoine watched as the king was transformed into a tree before his eyes. He reached out and felt what had been Dagobert's arm, but it was coarse and scratchy under his fingertips. From somewhere deep inside the new tree he heard a low groan, but the noise was quickly lost in the breeze.

Antoine fled, running until he collapsed. When he woke, the Woodland Flower unicorn stood over him once more. It nudged him with its nose, as if to offer him a ride. After a day's journey they reached the forest's edge and the gates of the Château de Temps. A crowd had gathered, expecting the king's return, but they saw that Antoine was alone, riding the magnificent unicorn.

When Antoine explained what had happened, the people gasped. They knew the dangers of attempting to steal golden leaves from the enchanted forest and that, like many others before him, Dagobert would be trapped there for thousands of years.

The Woodland Flower unicorn bowed its head. "Take these flowers from my mane and restore the château to what it once was," it commanded. An old woman stepped forward from the crowd. She took the flowers, twisted their stems into a coronet and placed it on Antoine's head. The loyal servant became king and the people cheered.

The Lore of Woodland Flowers

UNIQUE QUALITY

Woodland Flowers are gentle, kind and
have a deep affinity with other animals.

HORNS

Their curled horns have a gnarled, antler-like texture.

APPEARANCE

They have brown, velvety coats and
manes bejewelled with wild flowers.

HABITAT

They can be found deep within the
wildest woodlands and forests.

MAGIC

Telepathy • Flowers in their manes have
restorative powers • Can influence the weather

WISDOM

Woodland Flowers represent justice
and fidelity. They are also
associated with royalty.

A BRIEF HISTORY OF UNICORNS

Eons ago
The Gold Unicorn and the Silver Unicorn spring into existence. (page 23)

Ancient Egypt
Pharaohs fail to capture Desert Flames. Instead, scholars study the magical creatures. (pages 9–10)

1577
Luca di Bosco and Alessandra Massima found the Magical Unicorn Society. (page 49)

1868
Chester Lewis discovers that the Ancient Greeks worshipped Shadow Nights. (page 109)

1872
Mariana de Fey records unicorn hoof prints, making tracking easier. (page 79)

930

Mandu triumphs at the Battle of the Shining Jewels, thanks to the power of unicorns. (page 38)

975

Fatima Musa encounters a Desert Flame unicorn. (page 72)

Medieval France

King Dagobert encounters a Woodland Flower. (page 59)

1050

Thora the Brave rescues an Ice Wanderer, and later becomes queen. (page 87)

1900

Miranda Martinez publishes her definitive essay on the different ways in which unicorns communicate. (page 67)

1999

Selwyn E. Phipps becomes president of the Magical Unicorn Society. (page 6)

How to COMMUNICATE WITH UNICORNS

The mysterious ways in which these magical creatures
communicate with each other and with human beings differs
from one unicorn family to the next. These observations
were documented by Miranda Martinez in 1900.

SONG

Woodland Flowers are the shyest
of the unicorn families, however,
according to folklore, humans
can summon them with song.

ELECTRICITY

Some Storm Chaser unicorns
can communicate via lightning
bolts, flashing across the sky.

TOUCH

If you get close enough to
touch a Mountain Jewel, you or
other unicorns can communicate
with them telepathically –
through thoughts instead
of sound or movement.

LIGHT

The Ice Wanderer unicorns
that live at the North and South
Poles communicate with each
other via colourful lights that
they shoot across the sky.

DREAMS

Shadow Night unicorns appear
in people's dreams, warning
them of potential danger.

Desert Flames

Fatima Musa loved animals. If she wasn't playing with her adored pet cats, lizards, birds and dogs, she could be found in the local market, watching closely as the farmers sold their goats, cows or camels. Little did she know that when she grew up, she would form a bond with one of the most extraordinary animals – a Desert Flame unicorn.

Fatima lived in a bustling town in 10th-century Persia, where nearly anything and everything animal-related was available to buy. Traders would sell long-legged buzzards, leopards, and a myriad of colourful geckos and emerald-eyed snakes. Even river-dwelling crocodiles could be purchased for the right price.

Fatima was enthralled by the variety of creatures and spent hours sketching them. Her wonderful drawings, with arabesque detailing around the outside, accompanied by handwritten, scientific notes, was the perfect training for her future. Fatima went on to become a famous explorer and the first person to chronicle a Desert Flame unicorn.

When Fatima was a young woman she joined a party of merchants who were travelling across the Great Salt Desert. Along the way she wanted to draw and catalogue what she found. She was soon on the trail of the gazelles, ground jays, and even the cheetahs that lived out on the desert plains. Every night she would crouch by the fire and record what she'd seen.

One evening, as Fatima was bundled up against the freezing night air in her canvas tent, the wind gathered a strength and pace never seen before. She hunkered down as low to the ground as she could, wrapping her blankets tightly around her shoulders. However, the whistling of the wind grew to a roar, and Fatima's canvas tent was ripped away completely.

The rest of the camp was in chaos, too. Men and women struggled to control the camels, which were braying loudly. The merchants tried their best to gather up their goods that were strewn across the desert. Fatima tried in vain to gather up her own things, but everything was lost to the wind. She blindly turned towards a voice that had shouted out to her, but she couldn't see her hand in front of her face. She stumbled and fell. Her whole world went black.

Hours later, Fatima woke and found to her horror that her travelling companions were gone. She called out, but her voice only echoed across the desert. She tried not to panic. She would head east, towards home, working the direction out by the position of the Sun. It was hard going. As noon approached, Fatima was baking in the heat. The sweat dripped down her face. She would have given all her meagre possessions for one sip of water. She knelt down on the ground in despair, and let the sand sift between her fingers. "Someone help me," she cried out – and that's when she saw it …

There was a strange light shimmering in the distance, as if the Sun was reflecting off polished metal. Fatima rubbed her eyes, convinced it was a mirage. She saw another flash of light, and then another ... Moving towards her were what looked like a group of horses, but these were like none she'd ever seen before. It was a blessing of unicorns – rare creatures she had only heard of in stories.

The lead unicorn bent down and nudged her with its nose. It snorted and stamped its foot gently. It had deep brown eyes, a tawny brown-blonde coat, and a magnificent twisting horn. It encouraged Fatima to stand up.

By now the other unicorns had surrounded her. They all seemed curious, as if they'd never seen a human before. Fatima was far more curious though. She could sense that she was in the presence of something special – even magical. The unicorns were gentle but proud and had a sweet smell that reminded her of her grandmother's lemon tree.

The blessing crowded around her and gently nudged her in the direction they were travelling. Fatima was so enchanted that she walked alongside them, being careful to keep her distance from their shiny bronze horns. They looked like they had the potential to cause some serious harm.

Eventually, the unicorns led her to an oasis deep in the desert. They gathered around a pool of water, which other animals were already joyfully lapping up. One unicorn used its horn to shake a date tree that soared above them, scattering the ground with juicy fruit. Gratefully, Fatima drank her fill of water and devoured the dates. When clouds gathered overhead once more, she took shelter as best she could among the blessing. But, eventually, the winds whipped up so fiercely that even the unicorns decided to flee.

As the sandstorm rolled towards them, one Desert Flame hurried over to Fatima and nudged her on to its back. Fatima grabbed hold of its tufty mane and the unicorn dashed onwards. It was the fastest creature she'd ever encountered. As the sand threatened to engulf them, the unicorns stamped their hooves. Fatima felt a strange, weightless feeling, and realized that the unicorn she was riding had lifted off the ground.

The unicorn was flying! Fatima saw the ground shrinking far beneath her. The unicorn's brass horn shone brightly and its hooves were glowing with a yellow-orange flame.

Exhausted, Fatima nestled into the unicorn's coat and slept. When she woke, the creature was putting her down gently. She looked around and recognized where she was – she was just outside her hometown. She patted the unicorn on the flank. It turned to go, and before she knew it, it was off once more, back to its family.

Once she was home, Fatima told her story to anyone who would listen. Of course, people were skeptical. She made drawings to try and show people what she'd seen, but they accused her of making things up. That was when she made the decision to become a professional explorer. She would find the Desert Flames again and prove people wrong.

Over the years, she returned to the desert many times and saw the magical unicorns. They remembered her and greeted her with delighted whinnies and gentle nuzzles. Remembering the time she had flown with them through the bright blue skies never failed to make her smile.

The Lore of Desert Flames

UNIQUE QUALITY

Desert Flames are the fastest unicorns in the world.

HORNS

Their horns are a shimmering bronze and twist
like the wind-swept sands of the desert.

APPEARANCE

They have light, sandy-brown coats with
flame-coloured manes and tails.

HABITAT

They live in arid deserts and dry,
rocky landscapes.

MAGIC

Can run at great speeds • Flight

WISDOM

Desert Flames are protective herd
animals and are renowned for
helping people in distress.

A Spotter's Guide to
TRACKING
UNICORNS

Unicorns are among the most elusive
creatures on Earth, and tracking them is
a tricky business. However, they do leave
clues behind if you know what to look for.

WHEN TO FIND UNICORNS

Unicorns can only be seen at certain times of the day or
night and certain times of the year. So you need to consider
when they're most active if you want to spot one.

STORM CHASERS

are closely linked to the
elements, and they are especially
active during extreme weather.

WATER MOONS

are especially active at twilight.
When the moon is rising, Water
Moons will be around.

ICE WANDERERS

rarely sleep, so can be seen
at all hours of the day, but they
particularly love the dead of
night, when temperatures
are at their coldest.

DESERT FLAMES

are most active at midday, when
the Sun is at its highest and the
air is hottest. At night, when
the desert cools, they huddle
together for warmth.

MOUNTAIN JEWELS

are early risers, waking at dawn.
They roam rocky mountainsides
in all weathers, rain or shine.

SHADOW NIGHTS

can only be seen in the dead
of night. To see these creatures,
you have to stay up very late.

WOODLAND FLOWERS

have never been seen during
winter, when they hibernate
in mossy caves. They return
to the woods in the spring.

IDENTIFY TRACKS

The unique hoof prints left by each unicorn family were documented by Society member Mariana de Fey. Here's a guide to the different tracks they make.

WATER MOONS

WOODLAND FLOWERS

DESERT FLAMES

ICE WANDERERS

SHADOW NIGHTS

MOUNTAIN JEWELS

STORM CHASERS

Unicorns live in
harmony with our
beautiful planet.

Ice Wanderers

Ice Wanderer unicorns live wherever it is
cold and snowy, from the frozen plains of Siberia
to the icy caps of the North and South Poles.
They are perfectly suited to cold conditions, with
their thick white coats providing great insulation
and camouflaging them from any potential
predators that might come their way.

Southern Ice Wanderers are completely white, with pearly coloured, twisted horns. They live in Antarctica and roam across its snowy plains in pairs. They swim in the icy waters and have been seen playing with other marine life, such as penguins and seals. Northern Ice Wanderers are more solitary. They are also white, but their manes are shinier and, in the right light, shimmer with a rainbow of colours. Their horns are smooth and made entirely out of ice. Sadly, if the Northern Ice Wanderers ever ventured into warmer climes, their horns would melt and they would die.

In both the high north and the low south, there is a phenomenon known as the Aurora Borealis or Aurora Australis. These are beautiful displays of lights that can be seen in the night sky, with colours ranging from bright greens to delicate pinks and dramatic reds. Some stories from Northern American cultures say that the lights are the spirits of the dead dancing across the skies. In Chinese folklore, the lights represent a heavenly battle between good and evil dragons. The Finnish tell stories of a fox that ran so quickly its tail caught fire and lit up the sky. Today, most scientists believe that the Aurora is produced when the upper atmosphere of the Earth is disturbed by solar winds, causing it to emit light and colour. But the members of the Magical Unicorn Society know that there is something else going on in those lights – something far more magical.

Years ago, I was trekking in the far north to conduct field research among Ice Wanderers. The unicorns of the northern ice caps live vast distances apart. There can't be more than twenty of them in the whole of the Arctic region. Yet these twenty unicorns always gather together at particular times of the year – during the summer and winter solstices. In the Arctic these are dramatic times. During the winter solstice it is dark all day, while on the day of the summer solstice it is light for a full twenty-four hours.

The Ice Wanderers meet on these two days and frolic together, as if they are exchanging news of the last six months and rekindling old friendships. They stomp their hooves in greeting. But I always wondered how they knew which day to arrive, and where to meet, and what it was they were 'saying' to each other. After all, these unicorns were silent, solitary creatures ...

... or so I had thought. Before the unicorns were due to meet for the winter solstice, I followed an Ice Wanderer to try and understand more. It took weeks of painstaking tracking, but what I saw was astonishing. When the sky was at its darkest, the unicorn I'd been following lifted up its head, and emitted a beautiful pink glow from its horn, sending the light ray shooting into the darkness. Then, after a second or two, a bright yellow

glow filled the sky as if in answer. This continued for several minutes – the pink and yellow glows shooting back and forth across the sky, lighting up the heavens.

Shortly after the display finished, another unicorn emerged from the snowy landscape, its horn glowing yellow. And all at once I understood the significance of the lights. The unicorns were communicating with each other with the light produced by their horns. It was a kind of celestial telepathy that explained how these unicorns interacted with each other over vast distances.

It also made me think of the special significance Ice Wanderers have in Norwegian folklore. For centuries, some people believed that the Aurora Borealis was associated with the Norse gods and goddesses they worshipped. These gods lived in a place called Asgard, which was joined to Earth by a rainbow bridge. The strange lights that sometimes filled the skies were thought to be reflections from the shields of the gods and goddesses crossing the rainbow bridge.

This myth was still widely believed in the time of a fearless queen called Thora the Brave. Tragedy befell Thora because she had the audacity to be born first in line to the throne, at a time when only men were allowed to inherit the kingdom. Her younger brother, Grim, wanted the throne for himself and, when the old king died, he seized it. Thora, who was only fifteen, was banished to the frozen wastelands, where she was left wandering for years with a small band of loyal followers. Each morning when she woke, Thora vowed that the time would come when she would return to the castle of her birth and take back her rightful throne.

One day, Thora and her followers were out hunting for seals when they saw colourful lights shoot across the sky. Thinking it was caused by the Norse gods and goddesses, they continued hunting. But instead of seals, they found an Ice Wanderer unicorn trapped between two rocks in a giant, glacial ice flow. The creature was struggling and whinnying in distress. Bright, coloured lights were shooting from its horn. The unicorn grew even more skittish and nervous when Thora approached, but she soothed it with her gentle voice. She freed the creature and nursed it for days while it regained its strength. After that, a special bond was sealed between the girl and the unicorn. The Ice Wanderer travelled everywhere with Thora.

On the day of the next summer solstice, when the Sun shone at midnight and the day was at its longest, Thora knew it was time to try to retake her throne. She had become a strong, resilient leader and an accomplished fighter. Moreover, she was carried into battle against her brother on the back of a near-invincible Ice Wanderer. When Thora raised her sword it shone with the colours of the Aurora Borealis, pulsing with an unearthly energy, and it smote down all before her.

Despite a long struggle and many losses on both sides, Thora emerged victorious. She threw her disloyal brother into a dungeon and became queen. She reigned justly and mercifully for sixty years with the Ice Wanderer always by her side. When Thora eventually succumbed to old age, the unicorn disappeared back into the wilderness and was never seen again.

After that, the Ice Wanderer became a symbol of strength, resilience and justice throughout the northern hemisphere. Thora is the only human known to have made a strong bond with one of these unicorns. They have so rarely been seen since those times that the old stories have become legends, and some people doubt their existence. Fortunately, I have seen them with my own eyes.

The Lore of Ice Wanderers

UNIQUE QUALITY

Ice Wanderers create beautiful
light displays across the sky.

HORNS

Northern Ice Wanderers have smooth horns of ice and
Southern Ice Wanderers have twisted horns of pearl.

APPEARANCE

These unicorns have white, sparkling coats with
cream-coloured manes and tails. The manes of Northern Ice
Wanderers can shine with rainbow colours in the right light.

HABITAT

They live in cold, snowy climates.

MAGIC

Communicate through magical
light • Near-invincible strength

WISDOM

Ice Wanderers stand for resilience and
fortitude in the face of hardship.

THE QUALITIES OF UNICORNS

Though the seven families of unicorn differ in their magical powers and in appearance, there are some qualities that all unicorns share.

MAGIC

Each and every unicorn is imbued with magic, from sparkling horn to tail.

GRACE

Unicorns are graceful creatures that move with elegant balance and poise.

LOYALTY

Unicorns are faithful to the members of their blessing, and occasionally form strong bonds with humans.

KINDNESS

Unicorns avoid confrontation, rarely harm humans and go out of their way to help other creatures.

POWER

Unicorns are naturally strong and resilient.

STARGAZING

Look up at the night sky and you will see that unicorns are in the stars. They're represented as a constellation (a collection of stars) called 'Monoceros', which literally means 'One Horn'. You can find it nestling between three famous constellations – Orion (the hunter), Canis Major (the greater dog) and Canis Minor (the lesser dog).

Orion

Canis
Minor

Monocerus

Canis
Major

Storm Chasers

The dramatic nature of Storm Chaser unicorns
is such that many Society members have stories
about them. At any meeting anecdotes abound:
"I saw one stamp its feet, and the heavens trembled
and a thunderstorm began to brew."
"I have proved that their blazing yellow tails
conduct electricity."
"Did you know that their cries can unleash
torrential rain?"

Many tales about Storm Chasers sound outlandish but, in my experience, most of them are true. These are incredibly powerful unicorns, with amazing abilities to affect the weather.

There are four main types of Storm Chaser unicorns, which are all found in Central and South America. Firstly, there are the Sunshine unicorns, known for their buttercup-yellow coats and sunflower-yellow manes and tails. They have horns made of star-lemon quartz, a light yellow precious gem. On cold and gloomy days these horns light up like the Sun and cast a warm glow that immediately increases the temperature. Sunshine unicorns have come to represent happiness and hope.

Next, there are the Shifters. The appearance of these unicorns literally changes with the weather. In bright sunlight, they shine yellow. In the rain, their colouring shifts to dark grey with cloud-white spots. In high winds, their colour can change quickly and dramatically, from brown to purple to light blue. They can be identified by their horns, which are made of jade and can appear green, yellow or pale purple depending on the weather. Shifters are associated with strong, but changeable, emotions.

Thirdly, there are the Snow unicorns. They live high up in the Central American mountains. They are stout and tough, with bright white coats and grey manes and tails. Their horns are made of stone and their hooves are as strong as iron. They are quick-tempered and, when they stomp their hooves on the ground in anger, they can cause deafening thunder. They represent tenacity.

Storm unicorns, after which the whole family are named, are large and slender with dove-grey coats. They have neon-yellow manes and tails that crackle with electric charge. Their horns, which are made of cloudy-grey opal, act like lightning conductors. When electric bolts flash down from the skies and strike a Storm's horn it will spark with electricity. They can use their horns to protect creatures from the deadly bolts. These unicorns can be found predominantly in Central America but occasionally wander north, particularly to places that experience extreme weather conditions. They represent passion and energy.

Once I travelled to Lake Maracaibo in Venezuela, where these Storm Chaser unicorns are often spotted. The weather in this area is constantly changing and fierce lightning storms are particularly frequent. On average, there are storms on two hundred and sixty days of the year there. People say that lightning doesn't strike in the same place twice, but at Lake Maracaibo I discovered that it certainly does.

While I was at Lake Maracaibo, I stayed with a local family. They told me the legend that explains exactly how Storm Chaser unicorns cause extreme weather. It tells of a blessing that included four young unicorns. Each of the four unicorns was a different type of Storm Chaser. There was a Sunshine, a Shifter, a Snow and a Storm, and it was their job to keep the sky in place. Each unicorn held one corner of the sky in its mouth, from the highest clouds down to the horizon, stretching the sky over the land like the canvas of a giant tent.

Unfortunately, the young unicorns were playful and mischievous. Instead of doing their duty, they preferred to play. The Storm unicorn, who was the oldest, led his friends into mischief again and again. Sunshine, Snow and Shifter would drop their corners of the sky and follow him – hence the name, Storm Chasers. When they stomped their hooves and chased each other's tails the sky would flutter and fall to the ground and bursts of lightning would fill the air. They had so much energy and so little patience that they never stayed holding the sky for long.

Now, let me tell you about my own encounter with Storm Chaser unicorns. My hosts at Lake Maracaibo told me about the unicorns in the area and showed me where I could observe them for myself. I packed a bag and, before dawn, I set off on foot to track them. Before long, I saw a Sunshine unicorn by the shores of the great lake. Sunshines are particularly active in the morning and so are easy to spot. I was able to create quite a detailed drawing before it scampered away.

I settled myself down and waited, and waited, and waited for another sighting ... I began to curse my luck, thinking that I had arrived on the one day without lightning. Just as I was beginning to despair, a spectacular flash of light tore across the sky. Then I heard the deepest rumble of thunder and a cataclysmic storm began. I took shelter and sat patiently. Within minutes, a Storm unicorn approached, with its deep grey coat and mane flickering with electricity. It was soon followed by others.

I moved forwards gingerly, trying not to startle them. Surprisingly, they let me get within an arm's length of them. I put out my hand to stroke the nose of one unicorn, when a lightning bolt flashed down from the sky. I felt the jolt go through me and I was thrown back, landing with a dull thud. For a minute or so I must have blacked out, but when I regained consciousness I saw that the

Storm unicorns were standing above me. They were crackling with electricity. Somehow they had shielded me from the worst of the strike, and thus saved my life. They waited with me while I got to my feet, then walked me back to the village, continuing to protect me from danger. The mix of the lightning strike and the unicorn magic in the air was a strange one. The hairs on my neck tingled, the tips of my fingers were fizzing and I could trace patterns in the air like a sparkler. Magical energy was coming off me in tiny, bright bolts.

When I returned, the family I was staying with were shocked by what had happened, but they were not surprised that the Storm unicorns had helped me. I showed them the strange sparks I could shoot from my fingers at will. They christened me 'Electric', and I've proudly used it as my middle name ever since. Sadly, I didn't keep my magical ability. It faded away after a few days, which is a shame because the members of the Magical Unicorn Society would have enjoyed the firework show.

The Lore of Storm Chasers

UNIQUE QUALITY

Storm Chasers are the only unicorn family
that has complete control over the elements.

HORNS

Their horns can vary – from star-yellow
quartz and jade to opal and stone.

APPEARANCE

The colour of their coats also varies, depending on
the type of Storm Chaser. Some are storm-cloud grey
or lightning yellow while others are snowy white.

HABITAT

Storm Chasers are usually found in Central America,
living by lakes or under the shadow of mountains.

MAGIC

Alter the weather • Create thunder and
lightning • Conduct electricity

WISDOM

Storm Chasers are associated with elemental
forces and represent strong emotions,
such as passion and anger.

UNICORN BELIEFS AND SUPERSTITIONS

The magical powers of unicorns form the basis of
many superstitions and beliefs around the world.

MAKE A WISH

If you throw a perfectly round pebble into a pond, you can make a wish
on a unicorn. It's particularly helpful for bringing good health and wellbeing.

PHOTOGRAPHY

Unicorns won't appear in
photographs – the only images of
them are drawings and sketches.
It's bad luck to try and capture
a unicorn on camera.

RAINBOWS

Many cultures believe that
unicorns and rainbows are
linked. People believe that if
you see a rainbow, it is likely
that your guardian unicorn
(see p.114-115) is nearby.

MIRRORS

If you see an unexplained shadow pass across a mirror, it could mean a Shadow Night is near. They can move between the dream world and the waking world, and can also be reflected in glass and water.

GEMSTONES

Opals, rubies and emeralds carry the spirit of Mountain Jewel unicorns inside them. Wearing these gemstones will bring you good luck, strength and resilience.

FLAME

Lighting a fire at midnight can bring a new Desert Flame unicorn into the world.

SOLAR ECLIPSE

A solar eclipse not only means you are more likely to see a unicorn, it also heightens their magical powers. Some say that even the Gold Unicorn and the Silver Unicorn can be seen on the days of a full solar eclipse.

Shadow
Nights

Since the earliest days of the Society,
there has been much debate over the
existence of Shadow Nights. Though
all unicorns are rare and difficult
to find, Shadow Nights are the
most mysterious. In unicorn
circles today, they are still
spoken of in hushed tones.

Over the years, many renowned members of the Magical Unicorn Society claim to have heard of rumours about Shadow Nights, but evidence of their existence could never be produced. Descriptions of the creatures have always been vague. Members of the Society all over the world have tried to pin down exactly where the creatures live, but it seems they exist everywhere and nowhere at once. All I can conclude is that they are unlike the six other unicorn families, who have tangible forms. Shadow Nights are in fact ethereal beings, made of pure magic, so they can exist in the spirit world as well as the earthly realm.

Maybe one of the reasons that Shadow Nights are so hard to describe is because they are only visible at night and, even then, they appear as shadowy beings without solid form. This explains why Shadow Nights often appear in people's dreams. It is said that they can cross the boundary between the dream world and the waking world. They heal the sick, dispel nightmares and plant ideas in people's minds that help them work through their problems.

I first experienced a Shadow Night vision when I was trekking through the South American jungle. I had been on the trail of an eighth unicorn family – a mission which ultimately proved fruitless. As I made my way back to camp, I began to feel ill. My temperature rocketed and I began sweating profusely. The trees seemed to swim in front of me.

My guide told me I was dangerously ill and that I should rest. So I made myself as comfortable as possible in the shade of a large tree. For the entire day I slipped in and out of consciousness, hardly aware of my surroundings. It was one of the most terrible days of my life and I wished more than anything for a healing, deep sleep. Mercifully, the Sun did eventually dip below the horizon and the jungle cooled a fraction as night descended.

That was when things became really strange. In the dark I saw something moving, approaching through the trees. It was certainly a unicorn, but one unlike any I had ever seen. Its coat was deep black, flecked with small spots of white and yellow, like a star-filled sky. On its head was an onyx horn, so dark that it reflected almost no light from the moon. It moved through the forest soundlessly, with the stealth of a master burglar. I tried to alert my companions, who were having supper nearby, but when I opened my mouth no sound came out. Not only could they not hear my attempted cries, I realized that they couldn't see the unicorn either.

Somehow I knew that a Shadow Night unicorn was approaching me. It glided closer. Its silvery mane rippled and its dark body seemed to roil with magical energy. It came so close to where I lay that I thought it would trample me, but instead it passed straight through my body. It was the most otherworldly experience I'd ever had. But I wasn't scared. I felt calm in its presence. It leant its great head against my cheek and whinnied softly. That was when I fell into a deep sleep and dreamt that the Shadow Night showed me a path out of the jungle.

The next morning I woke up refreshed. I felt better than I had since I was a much younger man, despite having feared certain death from the fever the day before. My mind was clear and I felt strong and full of energy. I told my friends what had happened. Even though they were all members of the Magical Unicorn Society, they were a little skeptical. How was it that they hadn't seen the Shadow Night if it had walked right past them? I didn't have an answer. All I knew was that I'd seen the unicorn both while I was awake and in my dreams. I was certain that it had saved my life. And if further proof were needed, I was able to lead our team through the jungle to safety, taking the route the unicorn had showed me in my dreams.

When I returned to London, I went straight to Silver Square where the Magical Unicorn Society's vast library is housed. For days, I searched the shelves for accounts of Shadow Night sightings. Finally I stumbled across what looked like an old diary – full of tightly packed writing and beautiful drawings. It had belonged to one of our former American members, an historian named Chester Lewis. Writing around one hundred and fifty years ago, he described an archaeological dig he had been working on in Greece. He was part of a team of Society members that discovered a stone carving of a horse's head buried deep in a temple. He suspected that a horn may once have protruded from the horse's brow, but had been snapped off years ago.

After conducting further research, he concluded that the Ancient Greeks had worshipped the Shadow Nights. They believed that if they called upon the unicorns in their dreams, they would be granted all sorts of favours, such as victory in battles, medical miracles and incredible riches. The Greeks decorated vases with the likenesses of Shadow Night unicorns and built temples in their honour. Chester recorded everything he found in great detail.

However, only a few weeks into the dig, things began to go wrong. One worker fell into a recently dug hole and badly injured herself. A researcher came down with a deadly fever and was plagued by visions of a raging fire. Birds and animals did not venture near the site of the excavations. Chester became worried and eventually he went to consult a local professor.

She told him that local people believed the temple was cursed. Apparently, long ago, an evil king had tried to capture a Shadow

Night unicorn – and had succeeded. He imprisoned it inside a large earthenware pot, keeping it as his pet. The king believed he could force the unicorn to grant his every wish. He was gravely mistaken. Instead, when the unicorn eventually broke free, famine and pestilence ravaged the land. The cruelty and ignorance of the king's actions had unleashed a nightmare into the world, and the whole kingdom was destroyed.

Chester Lewis didn't know what to make of the professor's story. As a Magical Unicorn Society member, he had never heard of a unicorn using its magic to harm humans. Mysteriously, his diary ended abruptly. According to his colleagues, one morning he returned to the dig site one last time to try and uncover the truth. That day, the site was destroyed by a terrible fire, and the temple ruins were lost to the world. Chester's diary was posted back to the Society anonymously, and he was never seen again. His diary remains in the Silver Square library to this day.

Whatever may have happened, it is clear that Shadow Nights have devastating and mysterious powers. Chester's story reminds us that unicorns, like all wild creatures, should be treated with respect and never underestimated. I am convinced, however, that the Shadow Night I met in the jungle saved my life, and that we still have much to learn about these strange and elusive unicorns.

The Lore of Shadow Nights

UNIQUE QUALITY

Shadow Nights are ethereal beings and
the only unicorns made of pure magic.

HORNS

Their horns are made of black onyx.

APPEARANCE

Shadow Nights are intangible creatures. When they do
appear in physical form, their manes look silvery and their
coats are deep purple or black and flecked with stars.

HABITAT

These unicorns move between the spirit
world, the dream world and reality.

MAGIC

Ability to appear in dreams • Healing powers

WISDOM

Shadow Nights represent sleep
and the power of dreams.

GUARDIAN UNICORNS

Everyone has a guardian unicorn. These unicorns
are aligned to your unique energy and offer guidance,
protection and comfort. Discover which unicorn represents
you, then turn the page to find out what this means.

Keep calm and
throw something to
distract it so you
can run away.

On a voyage to
a tropical island
that is thought to
be uninhabited.

ON THE ISLAND
YOU ARE CORNERED
BY A HISSING
SNAKE. WHAT
DO YOU DO?

Devise an elaborate
way to trap the snake
so you can escape.

START

IF YOU WERE GOING
ON AN ADVENTURE,
WHERE WOULD YOU
CHOOSE TO GO?

Make a detailed plan
so you're ready for your
solo adventure.

On an expedition to
a remote glacier near
the North Pole.

THE JOURNEY
AHEAD IS GOING
TO BE TOUGH AND
THERE'S LOTS TO
ORGANIZE. WHAT
DO YOU DO?

Find a team of
people to help you.
Many hands make
light work.

YOU COME ACROSS A GROUP OF PEOPLE LIVING ON THE ISLAND. WHAT DO YOU DO?

You are polite and try to make friends with them.

WOODLAND FLOWER

You decide to keep exploring.

DESERT FLAME

THE WEATHER TURNS – IT MUST BE MONSOON SEASON. WHAT DO YOU DO?

Find shelter and wait for the rain to pass.

STORM CHASER

Enjoy the atmosphere of the storm.

You sit up late, counting the constellations in the sky.

ICE WANDERER

NIGHT BEGINS TO FALL ON THE GLACIER. HOW DO YOU SPEND YOUR FIRST EVENING?

You get cosy in your tent and fall asleep.

SHADOW NIGHT

YOU'VE MADE IT TO THE GLACIER. WHAT'S THE FIRST THING THAT YOU WANT TO DO?

Stay near the coast and watch for whales and penguins.

WATER MOON

Trek off into the snow and go ice climbing.

MOUNTAIN JEWEL

YOUR GUARDIAN UNICORN

If you see a rainbow, it is likely that your guardian unicorn is nearby. Discover which family your guardian unicorn belongs to on the previous page, then find out what it means below.

WOODLAND FLOWERS

Known for their calm, gentle ways and their affinity for trees and flowers. People aligned with Woodland Flowers are likely to be friendly, kind and enjoy nature.

DESERT FLAMES

Known for their speed, strength and for living in close-knit blessings. People aligned to Desert Flames seek adventure. They are strong-willed, loyal and tough.

STORM CHASERS

These unicorns have an affinity with the elements. People who have a Storm Chaser guardian relish challenges. They are likely to be passionate, quick-witted and feisty.

MOUNTAIN JEWELS

Tough, hardy herd animals, people represented by Mountain Jewels are loyal and courageous. They are social and enjoy the company of others.

SHADOW NIGHTS

These unicorns can appear in dreams. People represented by this unicorn family are imaginative, sensitive and creative. They drive new ideas forward.

WATER MOONS

These unicorns are mystical and mesmerizing. People represented by this type are selfless, thoughtful, clever and patient. They love being near water.

ICE WANDERERS

These unicorns tend to prefer their own company. People represented by these unicorns are good listeners. They are brave, smart and resilient.

Est. 1577

The

MAGICAL UNICORN SOCIETY

For years, the Magical Unicorn Society was a top-secret
organization, and we only ever had a handful of members
in each branch. We guarded the secrets of the unicorns
closely, and the criteria for joining the Society was strict.
Nowadays, the joining process is less rigid (prospective
applicants are no longer required to show proof of two
separate unicorn encounters, for example). There are
three basic steps, outlined on the following pages.

Step One: The Riddle

Can you solve the magical riddle of the unicorn?

I come in all shapes and sizes,
And can help in many ways,
From breaking open cacti,
To emitting shining rays.
I'll be your weapon in a fight,
And guide you during flight,
Sparkle in a storm,
And help to keep you warm.
I can be gnarled or twisted,
Hot or cold,
Made of pearl,
Or made of gold.
Without me, you'll never be,
A magical unicorn, roaming free.
What am I?

Step Two: The Oath

The Society has an oath that all
members must memorize, recite and obey:

By the magical strength of the Mountain Jewel,
And the heart of the Woodland Flower,
By the speed of the dashing Desert Flame,
By hooves, by horns, by power.

I swear to hold the secret close,
to protect unicorns of every variety,
I am proud to be an enchanted member
of the Magical Unicorn Society!

Step Three:
Joining The Society

Once you have solved 'The Riddle' and memorized 'The Oath', you are ready to be part of the Society.

Gold Membership:
The Eighth Unicorn Family

Becoming a Gold Member of the Society is the highest honour, and requires a bit of work. There is still a lot we don't know about unicorns and strong evidence exists to suggest that an eighth, undiscovered unicorn family lives in the world today. The society is working hard to conduct research into these unknown creatures, and we need your help.

What do you think the eighth unicorn family is? Join us in our search for the eighth unicorn family. Visit our website: magicalunicornsocietybook.com

ABOUT THE ILLUSTRATORS

The Magical Unicorn Society thanks the illustrators who have spent so much time researching the different species of unicorns in this official handbook in order to create beautiful and accurate representations of these magnificent creatures.

HARRY AND ZANNA GOLDHAWK

Harry and Zanna Goldhawk work from their seaside cottage in Cornwall, an area in which Woodland Flower unicorns are often spotted. Taking inspiration from nature, they illustrate beautiful books and design gorgeous products for their business, Papio Press. The Society believes their representations of the unicorn species are unrivalled.

HELEN DARDIK

The Society has long been a fan of Helen Dardik's work, in particular her ability to convey the beauty and magic of flora and fauna. Born by the Black Sea, Helen lived in Siberia for a time, in the realm of Ice Wanderers. She moved to Israel to study art and design, and now works as a designer and illustrator in Canada.